SCHOLASTIC
Phonics

The Travelling Shop

Published in the UK by Scholastic Education, 2022
Scholastic Distribution Centre, Bosworth Avenue, Tournament Fields, Warwick, CV34 6UQ
Scholastic Ireland, 89E Lagan Road, Dublin Industrial Estate, Glasnevin, Dublin, D11 HP5F

SCHOLASTIC and associated logos are trademarks and/or registered trademarks of Scholastic Inc.
www.scholastic.co.uk
© 2022 Scholastic Limited
1 2 3 4 5 6 7 8 9 2 3 4 5 6 7 8 9 0 1

Printed by Ashford Colour Press
The book is made of materials from well-managed, FSC-certifiedforests
and other controlled sources.

MIX
Paper from
responsible sources
FSC® C011748

A CIP catalogue record for this book is available from the British Library.

ISBN 978-0702-30903-8

Every effort has been made to trace copyright holders for the works reproduced in this publication,
and the publishers apologise for any inadvertent omissions.

Author
Catherine Baker
Editorial team
Rachel Morgan, Vicki Yates, Abbie Rushton, Liz Evans
Design team
Dipa Mistry, Justin Hoffmann, Andrea Lewis, We Are Grace
Illustrations
Csilla Köszeghy/Astound

Help your child to read!

This book practises words with more than one consonant next to each other, plus short vowel sounds (like '**cr**ash' or 'le**ft**').
Read these words with your child:

drink   **went**   **stuck**   **cross**   **help**

Your child may need help to read these common tricky words:

she   **to**   **one**   **of**   **the**   **I**   **some**   **they**   **were**
we   **you**   **said**   **come**

Before reading
- Look at the cover picture and read the title together. Read the back cover blurb to your child.
- Ask your child: *Where do you think this story is set? What kind of vehicle is the travelling shop?*

During reading
- If your child gets stuck on a word, remind them to sound it out and then blend the sounds to read the word: p-l-a-n-e-t, planet.
- If they are still stuck, show them how to read the word.
- Enjoy looking at the pictures together. Pause to talk about the story.

After reading
- Ask your child: *How do you think Mildred felt when she heard the footsteps? Why?*
- *How did Mildred say thank you to the aliens who helped her?*

Can you spot the chameleon on 6 pages?

Mildred had a travelling shop. She took food and drinks to far-off planets.

She went in her rocket, Rustbucket.

One morning, Mildred landed on planet Blip.

crash!

Rustbucket got a big dent!

One of the jets dropped off.

Mildred spotted some Blippers.
They were big and strong – and they
looked cross!

But they were not cross.

Can we help you?

They helped to fix Rustbucket!

"Thank you!" said Mildred.
She left them lots of food and drink.

Then she took off.

Come back soon!

Retell the story

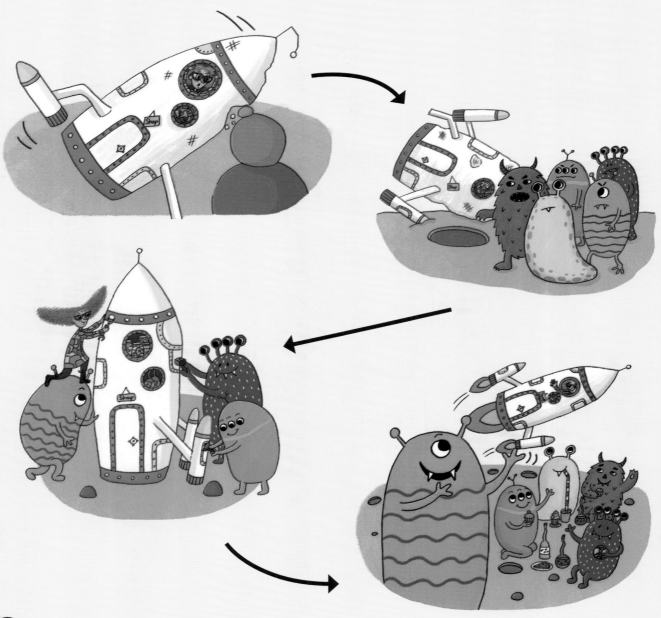